Rose and Rabbit Go Shopping

WANDA HOWELL
Illustrated by Dillon Oleny & Christine Olney

ISBN: 1508973563
ISBN-13: 978-1508973560

For Juanita
My sister, my friend, my shopping buddy
Special thanks to Clayton, my grandson, for suggesting that Rose and Rabbit go to town on a bike.

**Rose was reading the paper late one afternoon
when she noticed that school would be starting soon.**

"Rabbit," she said, "did you read the paper today?
BACK TO SCHOOL SALE is what it has to say.

It might just be exciting for us
to check out this back to school fuss."

"But Rose, we don't belong in class.
We are more comfortable out here in the grass."

"Yes, I know. That is exactly right.
But let's check out what I read here in black and white."

"You know, I wouldn't mind finding a nice little vest,
and a brand new hat would make you look your best!

How do you think we could get to town?
We don't have any way to get around.
After we drove the truck to the fair,
Farmer said we shouldn't be going anywhere!"

"Well now, the mailman goes just about everywhere.
I think, if we asked, he would take us there."

So, the next morning when the mailman drove up,
Rose asked her question. She spoke right up.
"Mr. Mailman, could you give us a ride?
We will sit very still once we get inside."

"I would be happy to have you along.
I might even sing you a little song.

I see some exciting things as I deliver the mail.
I even drive down an old Indian trail."

Sharing a ride with the mailman was fun
but soon they were longing to be out in the sun.

"Please stop here Mr. Mailman and let us get out.
We need to see what that bike is all about."

"The sign on the bike says FREE.
That is just right for Rabbit and me!"

"Biking to town will be such great fun.
I can't wait till we get some shopping done."

Rose and Rabbit went sailing along.
Farmer and his wife didn't realize they were gone.

They arrived at the store and went inside,
hoping not to end up having to hide.

Animals don't usually go to the store.
That's really not what animals are for.

Just as the two of them stepped in
they began to hear a very BIG din!

Horns and drums and lights galore
told them they were big winners there at the store.

They were the day's lucky customers you
see and had won a totally free shopping spree!

A shopping spree, completely free,
made them as happy as could be!

Instead of a brand new hat and a vest
they decided that jewelry would be best.

With bright gold chains around their necks
they wondered what would happen next.

Suddenly the manager of the store appeared
with bags of treats toward animals geared.

There were dog bones and carrots and other treats.
Everything was suited to bodies with four feet.

Finally it was time to get started for home.
They needed to get there while the sun still shone.

Just as they were ready to open the door
here came Farmer and his wife into the store.

"Oh, my goodness," said Farmer. "You have done it once more.
You have misbehaved just like before.
You have so many ideas going around in your head.
I'm not sure you've ever listened to what I've said.

Do you remember that after you drove to the fair
I said that you shouldn't be going anywhere?

Now, let's load all your things into the truck.
You can explain about the bike, with a little luck!"

Rose and Rabbit had enjoyed an adventurous day.
If you asked them about it they would have plenty to say!

That's all for this Time

Wanda Howell is a busy wife, mother and grandmother. She is a fabric artist who designs and pieces beautiful quilts. Wanda and her husband live near Columbia City, Indiana with an orange cat named Nelson. This is her third book about the adventures of Rose and Rabbit.

Dillon Olney grew up in Fort Wayne IN, he recently graduated from Indiana University with a BFA in sculpture. Dillon currently lives and works as an underwriter in Cincinnati with his loving wife Sarah and pursues his artistic interests from his home studio.

Christine Olney, Dillon's mother, has thoroughly enjoyed collaborating together with him to illustrate the Rose and Rabbit series. As a child, Dillon would watch his mom paint on their chairs, walls, and table. She always painted the many things he would find in nature. She now enjoys watching Dillon create, as she looks on in wonder.

42013567R00015

Made in the USA
Middletown, DE
12 April 2019